HORRID HENRY
Rocks

Francesca Simon spent her childhood on the beach
in California, and then went to Yale and Oxford
Universities to study medieval history and literature.
She now lives in London with her family. She has
written over 50 books and won the Children's
Book of the Year in 2008 at the Galaxy British Book
Awards for *Horrid Henry and the Abominable Snowman*.

There is a complete list of **Horrid Henry**
titles at the end of the book.

Visit Horrid Henry's website at
www.horridhenry.co.uk for competitions,
games, downloads and a monthly newsletter!

HORRID HENRY
Rocks

Francesca Simon
Illustrated by Tony Ross

Orion
Children's Books

ORION CHILDREN'S BOOKS

First published in Great Britain in 2010 by Orion Children's Books
This edition published in 2016 by Hodder and Stoughton

10

A CIP catalogue record for this book
is available from the British Library.

ISBN 978 1 4072 3918 7

Printed and bound in Great Britain
by Clays Ltd, St Ives plc

The paper and board used in this book are
made from wood from responsible sources.

Orion Children's Books
An imprint of
Hachette Children's Group
Part of Hodder and Stoughton
Carmelite House
50 Victoria Embankment
London EC4Y 0DZ

An Hachette UK Company
www.hachette.co.uk

www.hachettechildrens.co.uk
www.horridhenry.co.uk

For Jesse Nunn,
a major league Horrid Henry fan,
and for Imogen Stubbs

CONTENTS

1

HORRID HENRY'S INVASION

'Baa! Baa! Baa!'

Perfect Peter baaed happily at his sheep collection. There they were, his ten lovely little sheepies, all beautifully lined up from biggest to smallest, heads facing forward, fluffy tails against the wall, all five centimetres apart from one another, all—

Perfect Peter gasped. Something was wrong. Something was terribly wrong. But what? What? Peter scanned the mantelpiece. Then he saw . . .

Nooooo!

Fluff Puff, his favourite sheep, the one with the pink and yellow nose, was facing the wrong way round. His nose was shoved against the wall. His tail was facing forward. And he was . . . he was . . . crooked!

This could only mean . . . this could only mean . . .

'Mum!' screamed Peter. 'Mum! Henry's been in my room again!'

'Henry!' shouted Mum. 'Keep out of Peter's room.'

'I'm not in Peter's room,' yelled Horrid Henry. 'I'm in mine.'

'But he was,' wailed Peter.

'Wasn't!' bellowed Horrid Henry.

Tee hee.

Horrid Henry was strictly forbidden to go into Peter's bedroom without Peter's permission. But sometimes, thought Horrid Henry, when Peter was being

even more of a toady toad than usual,
he had no choice but to invade.

Peter had run blabbing to Mum that
Henry had watched *Mutant Max* and
Knight Fight when Mum had said he
could only watch one or the other.
Henry had been banned from watching
TV all day. Peter was such a telltale
frogface ninnyhammer toady poo bag,
thought Horrid Henry grimly. Well, just
wait till Peter tried to colour in his new
picture, he'd—

'MUM!' screamed Peter. 'Henry
switched the caps on my coloured pens.
I just put pink in the sky.'

'Didn't!' yelled Henry.

'Did!' wailed Peter.

'Prove it,' said Horrid Henry,
smirking.

Mum came upstairs. Quickly Henry
leapt over the mess covering the floor

of his room, flopped on his bed and grabbed a *Screamin' Demon* comic. Peter came and stood in the doorway.

'Henry's being horrid,' snivelled Peter.

'Henry, have you been in Peter's room?' said Mum.

Henry sighed loudly. 'Of course I've been in his smelly room. I live here, don't I?'

'I mean when he wasn't there,' said Mum.

'No,' said Horrid Henry. This wasn't a lie, because even if Peter *wasn't* there his horrible stinky smell was.

'He has too,' said Peter. 'Fluff Puff was turned the wrong way round.'

'Maybe he was just trying to escape from your pongy pants,' said Henry. '*I* would.'

'Mum!' said Peter.

'Henry! Don't be horrid. Leave your brother alone.'

'I *am* leaving him alone,' said Horrid Henry. 'Why can't he leave *me* alone? And get out of *my* room, Peter!' he shrieked, as Peter put his foot just inside Henry's door.

Peter quickly withdrew his foot.

Henry glared at Peter.

Peter glared at Henry.

Mum sighed. 'The next one who goes into the other's room without permission will be banned from the computer for a week. And no pocket money either.'

She turned to go.

Henry stuck out his tongue at Peter.

'Telltale,' he mouthed.

'Mum!' screamed Peter.

Perfect Peter stalked back to his bedroom. How dare Henry sneak in and mess up his sheep? What a mean, horrible brother. Perhaps he needed to calm down and listen to a little music. The *Daffy and her Dancing Daisies Greatest Hits* CD always cheered him up.

'Dance and prance. Prance and dance.

You say moo moo. We say baa.

Everybody says moo moo baa baa,'
piped Perfect Peter as he put on the
Daffy CD.

Boils on your fat face
Boils make you dumb.
Chop Chop Chop 'em off
Stick 'em on your bum!

blared the CD player.

Huh? What was that horrible song?
Peter yanked out the CD. It was the
Skullbangers singing the horrible 'Bony
Boil' song. Henry must have sneaked a
Skullbanger CD inside the Daffy case.
How dare he? How dare he? Peter
would storm straight downstairs and
tell Mum. Henry would get into big
trouble. Big big trouble.

Then Peter paused. There *was* the
teeny-tiny possibility that Peter had

mixed them up by mistake . . . No.
He needed absolute proof of Henry's
horridness. He'd do his homework, then
have a good look around Henry's room
to see if his Daffy CD was hidden there.

Peter glanced at his 'To Do' list
pinned on his noticeboard. When he'd
written it that morning it read:

Peter's To Do List
Practise Cello
Fold clothes and put away
Do homework
Brush my teeth
Read Bunny's Big Boo Boo

The list now read:

Peter's To Do List
Practise ~~cello belly~~ belly dancing
unFold clothes and ~~put away~~ throw
Don't ~~do~~ do homework
~~Flush~~ my teeth ~~down the toilet~~
Read Bunny's Big ~~Poo Poo~~

At the bottom someone had added:

Pick my nose
Pinch mum
Give Henry all my money

Well, here was proof! He was going to go straight down and tell on Henry.

'Mum! Henry's been in my room again. He scribbled all over my To Do list.'

'Henry!' screamed Mum. 'I am sick and tired of this! Keep out of your brother's bedroom! This is your last warning! No playing on the computer for a week!'

Sneak. Sneak. Sneak.

Horrid Henry slipped inside the enemy's bedroom. He'd pay Peter back for getting him banned from the computer.

There was Peter's cello. Ha! It was the work of a moment to unwind all the strings. Now, what else, what else? He could switch around Peter's pants and sock drawers.

No! Even better. Quickly Henry undid all of Peter's socks, and mismatched them. Who said socks should match?

Tee hee. Peter would go mad when he found out he was wearing one Sammy the Snail sock with one Daffy sock. Then Henry snatched Bunnykins off Peter's bed and crept out.

Sneak. Sneak. Sneak.

Perfect Peter crept down the hall and stood outside Henry's bedroom, holding a muddy twig. His heart was pounding. Peter knew he was strictly forbidden to go into Henry's room without permission. But Henry kept breaking

11

that rule. So why shouldn't he?

Squaring his shoulders, Peter tiptoed in.

Crunch.

Crunch.

Crunch.

Henry's room was a pigsty, thought Perfect Peter, wading through broken knights, crumpled sweet wrappers, dirty clothes, ripped comics, and muddy shoes.

Mr Kill. He'd steal Mr Kill. Ha! Serve Henry right. And he'd put the muddy twig in Henry's bed. Serve him double right. Perfect Peter grabbed Mr Kill, shoved the twig in Henry's bed and nipped back to his room.

And screamed.

Fluff Puff wasn't just turned the wrong way, he was – gone! Henry must have stolen him. And Lambykins was

gone too. And Squish. Peter only had seven sheep left. 🐑 🐑 🐑 🐑 🐑 🐑 🐑

And where was his Bunnykins? He wasn't on the bed where he belonged. No!!!!!! This was the last straw. This was war.

The coast was clear. Peter always took ages having his bath. Horrid Henry slipped into the worm's room.

He'd pay Peter back for stealing Mr
Kill. There he was, shoved at the top of
Peter's wardrobe, where Peter always
hid things he didn't want Henry to find.
Well, ha ha ha, thought Horrid Henry,
rescuing Mr Kill.

Now what to do, what to do?
Horrid Henry scooped up all of Peter's
remaining sheep and shoved them inside
Peter's pillowcase.

What else? Henry glanced round Peter's immaculate room. He could mess it up. Nah, thought Henry. Peter loved tidying. He could – aha.

Peter had pinned drawings all over the wall above his bed. Henry surveyed them. Shame, thought Henry, that Peter's pictures were all so dull. I mean, really, 'My Family', and 'My Bunnykins'. Horrid Henry climbed on Peter's bed to reach the drawings.

Poor Peter, thought Horrid Henry. What a terrible artist he was. No wonder he was such a smelly toad if he had to look at such awful pictures all the time. Perhaps Henry could improve them . . .

Now, let's see, thought Horrid Henry, getting out some crayons. Drawing a crown on my head would

be a big improvement. There! That
livens things up. And a big red nose on
Peter would help, too, thought Henry,
drawing away. So would a droopy
moustache on Mum. And as for that
stupid picture of Bunnykins, well,
why not draw a lovely toilet for him
to—

'What are you doing in here?' came
a little voice.

Horrid Henry turned.

There was Peter, in his bunny
pyjamas, glaring at him.

Uh oh. If Peter told on him again,
Henry would be in big, big, mega-big
trouble. Mum would probably ban him
from the computer for ever.

'You're in my room. I'm telling on
you,' shrieked Peter.

'Shhh!' hissed Horrid Henry.

'What do you mean, shhh?' said

16

Peter. 'I'm going straight down to tell Mum.'

'One word and you're dead, worm,' said Horrid Henry. 'Quick! Close the door.'

Perfect Peter looked behind him.

'Why?'

'Just do it, worm,' hissed Henry.

Perfect Peter shut the door.

'What are you doing?' he demanded.

'Dusting for fingerprints,' said Horrid Henry smoothly.

Fingerprints?

'What?' said Peter.

'I thought I heard someone in your room, and ran in to check you were okay. Just look what I found,' said Horrid Henry dramatically, pointing to Peter's now empty mantelpiece.

Peter let out a squeal.

'My sheepies!' wailed Peter.

'I think there's a burglar in the
house,' whispered Horrid Henry
urgently. 'And I think he's hiding . . .
in your room.'

Peter gulped. A burglar? In his room?
'A burglar?'

'Too right,' said Henry. 'Who do you
think stole Bunnykins? And all your
sheep?'

'You,' said Peter.

Horrid Henry snorted. 'No! What
would I want with your stupid sheep?

18

But a sheep rustler would love them.'

Perfect Peter hesitated. Could Henry be telling the truth? *Could* a burglar really have stolen his sheep?

'I think he's hiding under the bed,' hissed Horrid Henry. 'Why don't you check?'

Peter stepped back.

'No,' said Peter. 'I'm scared.'

'Then get out of here as quick as you can,' whispered Henry. *'I'll* check.'

19

'Thank you, Henry,' said Peter.

Perfect Peter crept into the hallway. Then he stopped. Something wasn't right . . . something was a little bit wrong.

Perfect Peter marched back into his bedroom. Henry was by the door.

'I think the burglar is hiding in your wardrobe, I'll get—'

'You said you were fingerprinting,' said Peter suspiciously. 'With what?'

'My fingers,' said Horrid Henry. 'Why do you think it's called *finger*printing?'

Then Peter caught sight of his drawings.

'You've ruined my pictures!' shrieked Peter.

'It wasn't me, it must have been the burglar,' said Horrid Henry.

'You're trying to trick me,' said Peter.

'I'm telling!'

Time for Plan B.

'I'm only in here 'cause you were in my room,' said Henry.

'Wasn't!'

'Were!'

'Liar!'

'Liar!'

'You stole Bunnykins!'

'You stole Mr Kill!'

'Thief!'

'Thief!'

'I'm telling on you.'

'I'm telling on you!'

Henry and Peter glared at each other.

'Okay,' said Horrid Henry. 'I won't invade your room if you won't invade mine.'

'Okay,' said Perfect Peter. He'd agree to anything to get Henry to leave his sheep alone.

Horrid Henry smirked.

He couldn't wait until tomorrow when Peter tried to play his cello . . . tee hee.

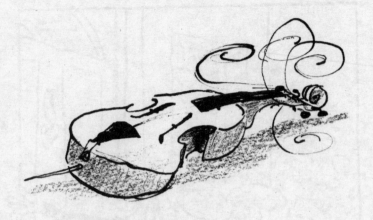

Wouldn't he get a shock!

2

MOODY MARGARET'S SLEEPOVER

'What are you doing here?' said Moody Margaret, glaring.

'I'm here for the sleepover,' said Sour Susan, glaring back.

'You were uninvited, remember?' said Margaret.

'And then you invited me again, remember?' snapped Susan.

'Did not.'

'Did too. You told me last week I could come.'

'Didn't.'

'Did. You're such a meanie, Margaret,' scowled Susan. Aaaarrggghh. Why was she friends with such a moody old grouch?

Moody Margaret heaved a heavy sigh. Why was she friends with such a sour old slop bucket?

'Well, since you're here, I guess you'd better come in,' said Margaret. 'But don't expect any dessert 'cause there won't be enough for you and my *real* guests.'

Sour Susan stomped inside Margaret's house. Grrrr. She wouldn't be inviting Margaret to her next sleepover party, that's for sure.

Horrid Henry couldn't sleep. He was hot. He was hungry.

'Biscuits!' moaned his tummy. 'Give me biscuits!'

Because Mum
and Dad were
the meanest,
most horrible
parents in the
world, they'd
forgotten to buy
more biscuits

and there wasn't a single solitary crumb
in the house. Henry knew because he'd
searched everywhere.

'Give me biscuits!' growled his
tummy. 'What are you waiting for?'

I'm going to die of hunger up here,
thought Horrid Henry. And it will be
all Mum and Dad's fault. They'll come
in tomorrow morning and find just a
few wisps of hair and some teeth. Then
they'd be sorry. Then they'd wail and
gnash. But it would be too late.

'How could we have forgotten to buy

chocolate biscuits?' Dad would sob.

'We deserve to be locked up forever!' Mum would shriek.

'And now there's nothing left of Henry but a tooth, and it's all our fault!' they'd howl.

Humph. Serve them right.

Wait. What an idiot he was. Why should he risk death from starvation when he knew where there was a rich stash of all sorts of yummy biscuits waiting just for him?

Moody Margaret's Secret Club tent was sure to be full to bursting with goodies! Horrid Henry hadn't raided it in ages. And so long as he was quick, no one would ever know he'd left the house.

'Go on, Henry,' urged his tummy. 'FEED ME!'

Horrid Henry didn't need to be urged twice.

Slowly, quietly, he sneaked out of bed, crept down

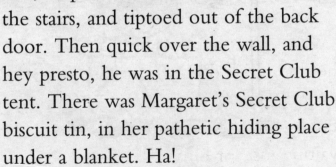

the stairs, and tiptoed out of the back door. Then quick over the wall, and hey presto, he was in the Secret Club tent. There was Margaret's Secret Club biscuit tin, in her pathetic hiding place under a blanket. Ha!

Horrid Henry prised open the lid. Oh wow. It was filled to the brim with

Chocolate Fudge Chewies! And those scrumptious Triple Chocolate Chip Marshmallow Squidgies! Henry scooped up a huge handful and stuffed them in his mouth.

Chomp. Chomp. Chomp.

Oh wow. Oh wow. Was there anything more delicious in the whole wide world than a mouthful of nicked biscuits?

'More! More! More!' yelped his tummy.

Who was Horrid Henry to say no?

Henry reached in to snatch another mega handful . . .

BANG! SLAM! BANG!

STOMP! STOMP! STOMP!

'That's too bad, Gurinder,' snapped Margaret's voice. 'It's my party so I decide. Hurry up, Susan.'

'I am hurrying,' said Susan's voice.

The footsteps were heading straight for the Secret Club tent.

Yikes. What was Margaret doing outside at this time of night? There wasn't a moment to lose.

Horrid Henry looked around wildly. Where could he hide? There was a wicker chest at the back, where Margaret kept her dressing-up clothes. Horrid Henry leapt inside and pulled the lid shut. Hopefully, the girls wouldn't be long and he could escape

31

home before Mum and Dad discovered he'd been out.

Moody Margaret bustled into the tent, followed by her mother, Gorgeous Gurinder, Kung-Fu Kate, Lazy Linda, Vain Violet, Singing Soraya and Sour Susan.

'Now, girls, it's late, I want you to go straight to bed, lights out, no talking,' said Margaret's mother. 'My little Maggie Moo Moo needs her beauty sleep.'

32

Ha, thought Horrid Henry. Margaret could sleep for a thousand years and she'd still look like a frog.

'Yes, Mum,' said Margaret.

'Good night, girls,' trilled Margaret's mum. 'See you in the morning.'

Phew, thought Horrid Henry, lying as still as he could. He'd be back home in no time, mission safely accomplished.

'We're sleeping out here?' said Singing Soraya. 'In a tent?'

'I said it was a Secret Club sleepover,' said Margaret.

Horrid Henry's heart sank. Huh? They were planning to sleep here? Rats rats rats double rats. He was going to have to hide inside this hot dusty chest until they were asleep.

Maybe they'd all fall asleep soon, thought Horrid Henry hopefully.

Because he had to get home before Mum and Dad discovered he was missing. If they realised he'd sneaked outside, he'd be in so much trouble his life wouldn't be worth living and he might as well abandon all hope of ever watching TV or eating another biscuit until he was an old, shrivelled bag of bones struggling to chew with his one tooth and watch telly with his magnifying glass and hearing aid. Yikes!

Horrid Henry looked grimly at the biscuits clutched in his fist. Thank goodness he'd brought provisions. He

might be trapped here for a very long time.

'Where's your sleeping bag, Violet?' said Margaret.

'I didn't bring one,' said Vain Violet. 'I don't like sleeping on the floor.'

'Tough,' said Margaret, 'that's where we're sleeping.'

'But I need to sleep in a bed,' whined Vain Violet. 'I don't want to sleep out here.'

'Well we do,' said Margaret.

'Yeah,' said Susan.

'I can sleep anywhere,' said Lazy
Linda, yawning.

'I'm calling my mum,' said Violet.
'I want to go home.'

'Go ahead,' said Margaret. 'We don't
need you, do we?'

Silence.

'Oh go on, Violet, stay,' said
Gurinder.

'Yeah, stay,' said Kung-Fu Kate.

'No!' said Violet, flouncing out of the
tent.

'Hummph,' said Moody Margaret.

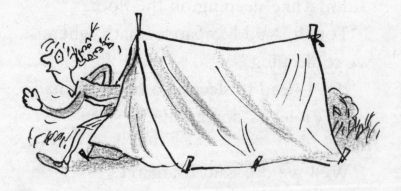

'She's no fun anyway. Now, everyone put your sleeping bags down where I say. I need to sleep by the entrance, because I need fresh air.'

'I want to sleep by the entrance,' said Soraya.

'No,' said Margaret, 'it's my party so I decide. Susan, you go at the back because you snore.'

'Do not,' said Susan.

'Do too,' said Margaret.

'Liar.'

'Liar.'

SLAP!

SLAP!

'That's it!' wailed Susan. 'I'm calling my mum.'

'Go ahead,' said Margaret, 'see if I care, snore-box. That'll be loads more Chocolate Fudge Chewies for the rest of us.'

37

Sour Susan stood still. She'd been looking forward to Margaret's sleepover for ages. And she still hadn't had any of the midnight feast Margaret had promised.

'All right, I'll stay,' said Susan sourly, putting her sleeping bag down at the back of the tent by the dressing-up chest.

'I want to be next to Gurinder,' said Lazy Linda, scratching her head.

'Do you have nits?' said Gurinder.

'No!' said Linda.

'You do too,' said Gurinder.

'Do not,' said Linda.

'Do too,' said Gurinder. 'I'm not sleeping next to someone who has nits.'

'Me neither,' said Kate.

'Me neither,' said Soraya.

'Don't look at me,' said Margaret. 'I'm not sleeping next to you.'

'I don't have nits!' wailed Linda.

'Go next to Susan,' said Margaret.

'But she snores,' protested Linda.

'But she has nits,' protested Susan.

'Do not.'

'Do not.'

'Nitty!'

'Snory!'

Suddenly something scuttled across
the floor.

'EEEEK!' squealed Soraya. 'It's

a mouse!' She scrambled onto the dressing-up chest. The lid sagged.

'It won't hurt you,' said Margaret.

'Yeah,' said Susan.

'Eeeek!' squealed Linda, shrinking back.

The lid sagged even more.

Cree—eaaak went the chest.

Aaarrrrggghhh, thought Horrid Henry, trying to squash himself down before he was squished.

'Eeeek!' squealed Gurinder, scrambling onto the chest.

CREE—EAAAAAK! went the chest.

Errrrgh, thought Horrid Henry, pushing up against the sagging lid as hard as he could.

'I can't sleep if there's a . . . mouse,' said Gurinder. She looked around nervously. 'What if it runs on top of my sleeping bag?'

Margaret sighed. 'It's only a mouse,' she said.

'I'm scared of mice,' whimpered Gurinder. 'I'm leaving!' And she ran out of the tent, wailing.

'More food for the rest of us,' said Margaret, shrugging. 'I say we feast now.'

'About time,' said Soraya.

'Let's start with the Chocolate Fudge Chewies,' said Margaret, opening the

41

Secret Club biscuit tin. 'Everyone can
have two, except for me, I get four
'cause it's my . . .'

Margaret peered into the tin. There
were only a few crumbs inside.

'Who stole the biscuits?' said
Margaret.

'Wasn't me,' said Susan.

'Wasn't me,' said Soraya.

'Wasn't me,' said Kate.

'Wasn't me,' said Linda.

Tee hee, thought Horrid Henry.

'One of you did, so no one is getting anything to eat until you admit it,' snapped Margaret.

'Meanie,' muttered Susan sourly.

'What did you say?' said Moody Margaret.

'Nothing,' said Susan.

'Then we'll just have to wait for the culprit to come forward,' said Margaret, scowling. 'Meanwhile, get in your sleeping bags. We're going to tell scary stories in the dark. Who knows a good one?'

'I do,' said Susan.

'Not the story about the ghost kitty-cat which drank up all the milk in your kitchen, is it?' said Margaret.

43

Susan scowled.

'Well, it's a true scary story,' said Susan.

'I know a real scary story,' said Kung-Fu Kate. 'It's about this monster—'

'Mine's better,' said Margaret. 'It's about a flesh-eating zombie which creeps around at night and rips off—'

'NOOOO,' wailed Linda. 'I hate being scared. I'm calling my mum to come and get me.'

'No scaredy-cats allowed in the Secret Club,' said Margaret.

'I don't care,' said Linda, flouncing out.

'It's not a sleepover unless we tell ghost stories,' said Moody Margaret. 'Turn off your torches. It won't be scary unless we're all sitting in the dark.'

Sniffle. Sniffle. Sniffle.

'I want to go home,' snivelled Soraya.

'I've never slept away from home
before . . . I want my mummy.'

'What a baby,' said Moody Margaret.

Horrid Henry was cramped and hot and
uncomfortable. Pins and needles were
shooting up his arm. He shifted his
shoulder, brushing against the lid.

There was a muffled creak.

Henry froze. Whoops. Henry prayed
they hadn't heard anything.

'. . . and the zombie crept inside
the tent gnashing its bloody teeth and
sniffing the air for human flesh, hungry
for more—'

Ow. His poor aching arm. Henry
shifted position again.

Creak . . .

'What was that?' whispered Susan.

'What was what?' said Margaret.

'There was a . . . a . . . creak . . .' said

Susan.

'The wind,' said Margaret. 'Anyway, the zombie sneaked into the tent and—'

'You don't think . . .' hissed Kate.

'Think what?' said Margaret.

'That the zombie . . . the zombie . . .'

I'm starving, thought Horrid Henry. I'll just eat a few biscuits really, really, really quietly—

Crunch. Crunch.

'What was that?' whispered Susan.

'What was what?' said Margaret. 'You're ruining the story.'

'That . . . crunching sound,' hissed Susan.

Horrid Henry gasped. What an idiot he was! Why hadn't he thought of this before?

Crunch. Crunch. Crunch.

'Like someone . . . someone . . . crunching on . . . bones,' whispered Kung-Fu Kate.

'Someone . . . here . . .' whispered Susan.

Tap. Horrid Henry rapped on the underside of the lid.

Tap! Tap! Tap!

'I didn't hear anything,' said Margaret loudly.

'It's the zombie!' screamed Susan.

'He's in here!' screamed Kate. 'AAAAARRRRRRRGHHHHHHH!'

'I'm going home!' screamed Susan and Kate. 'MUMMMMMMMMYYYY!' they wailed, running off.

Ha ha, thought Horrid Henry. His brilliant plan had worked!!! Tee hee. He'd hop out, steal the rest of the feast and scoot home. Hopefully Mum and Dad—

YANK!

Suddenly the chest lid was flung open and a torch shone in his eyes. Moody

48

Margaret's hideous face glared down at him.

'Gotcha!' said Moody Margaret. 'Oh boy, are you in trouble. Just wait till I tell on you. Ha ha, Henry, you're dead.'

Horrid Henry climbed out of the chest and brushed a few crumbs onto the carpet.

'Just wait till I tell everyone at school about your sleepover,' said Horrid Henry. 'How you were so mean and bossy everyone ran away.'

'Your parents will punish you forever,' said Moody Margaret.

'Your name will be mud forever,' said Horrid Henry. 'Everyone will laugh at you and serves you right, Maggie Moo Moo.'

'Don't call me that,' said Margaret, glaring.

49

'Call you what, Moo Moo?'

'All right,' said Margaret slowly. 'I won't tell on you if you give me two packs of Chocolate Fudge Chewies.'

'No way,' said Henry. 'I won't tell on you if you give me three packs of Chocolate Fudge Chewies.'

'Fine,' said Margaret. 'Your parents are still up, I'll tell them where you are right now. I wouldn't want them to worry.'

'Go ahead,' said Henry. 'I can't wait until school tomorrow.'

Margaret scowled.

'Just this once,' said Horrid Henry. 'I won't tell on you if you won't tell on me.'

'Just this once,' said Moody Margaret. 'But never again.'

They glared at each other.

When he was king, thought Horrid

Henry, anyone named Margaret would
be catapulted over the walls into an
oozy swamp. Meanwhile . . . on guard,
Margaret. On guard. I will be avenged!

3

HORRID HENRY'S AUTOBIOGRAPHY

Bang! Crash! Kaboom!

Rude Ralph bounced on a chair and did his Tarzan impression.

Moody Margaret yanked Lazy Linda's hair. Linda screamed.

Stone-Age Steven stomped round the room grunting 'Ugg.'

> **'Rat about town
> don't need a gown.
> Where I'm goin'
> Only fangs'll be showin,'**

shrieked Horrid Henry.

'Quiet!' barked Miss Battle-Axe.

'Settle down immediately.'

Ralph bounced.

Steven stomped.

Linda screamed.

Henry shrieked. He was the Killer
Boy Rats new lead singer, blasting
his music into the roaring crowd,
hurling—

'HENRY, BE QUIET!' bellowed
Miss Battle-Axe. 'Or playtime is
cancelled. For everyone.'

Horrid Henry scowled. Why oh why
did he have to come to school? Why
didn't the Killer Boy Rats start a school,
where you'd do nothing but scream and
stomp all day? Now that's the sort of
school everyone would want to go to.
But no. He had to come here. When
he was king all schools would just teach
jousting and spying and Terminator
Gladiator would be head.

Henry looked at the clock. How could it be only 9.42? It felt like he'd been sitting here for ages. What he'd give to be lounging right now on the comfy black chair, eating crisps and watching *Hog House* . . .

'Today we have a very exciting project,' said Miss Battle-Axe.

Henry groaned. Miss Battle-Axe's idea of an exciting project and his were never the same. An exciting project

55

would be building a time machine, or a
let's see who can give Henry the most
chocolate competition, or counting
how many times he could hit Miss
Battle-Axe with a water balloon.

'We'll be writing autobiographies,'
said Miss Battle-Axe.

Ha. He knew it would be something
boring. Horrid Henry hated writing.
All that pushing a pen across a piece
of paper. Writing always made his
hand ache. Writing was hard, heavy

work. Why did Miss Battle-Axe try to torture him every day? Didn't she have anything better to do? Henry groaned again.

'An autobiography means the story of your life,' continued Miss Battle-Axe, glaring at him with her evil red eyes. 'Everyone will write a page about themselves and all the interesting things they've done.'

Yawn. Could his life get any worse?

Write a page? A whole entire page? What could be more boring then writing on and on about himself—

Wait a minute.

He got to write . . . about himself? The world's most fascinating boy? He could write for hours about himself! Days. Weeks. Years. Hold on . . . what was batty old Miss Battle-Axe saying now?

'. . . the really exciting part is that our autobiographies will be published in the local newspaper next week.'

Oh wow! Oh wow! Oh wow! His autobiography would be published!

This was his chance to tell the world all about being Lord High Excellent Majesty of the Purple Hand Gang. How he'd vanquished so many evil enemies. All the brilliant tricks he'd played on Peter. He'd write about the Mega-Mean Time Machine. And the Fangmangler. And the millions of times he'd defeated the Secret Club and squished Moody Margaret to a pulp! And oh yes, he'd be sure to include the time he'd turned his one line in the school play into a starring part and scored the winning goal in the class football match. But one page would barely cover one day in his life.

He needed hundreds of pages . . . no, thousands of pages to write about just some of his top triumphs.

Where to begin?

'Let's start with you, Clare,' burbled Miss Battle-Axe. 'What would you put in your autobiography?'

Clare beamed. 'I walked when I was four months old, learned to read when I was two, did long division when I was three, built my first telescope when I was four, composed a symphony—'

'Thank you, Clare, I'm sure everyone will look forward to learning more about you,' said Miss Battle-Axe. 'Steven. What will—'

'Can't we just get started?' shouted Henry. 'I've got masses to write.'

'As I was saying, before I was so RUDELY interrupted,' said Miss Battle-Axe, glaring, 'Steven, what will you be writing about in your autobiography?'

'Being a caveman,' grunted Stone-Age Steven. 'Uggg.'

'Fascinating,' said Miss Battle-Axe. 'Bert! What's interesting about your life?'

'I dunno,' said Beefy Bert.

'DUNNO'

'Right, then, everyone get

to work,' said Miss Battle-Axe, fixing Horrid Henry with her basilisk stare.

Horrid Henry wrote until his hand ached. But he'd barely got to the time he tricked Margaret into eating glop before Miss Battle-Axe ordered everyone to stop.

'But I haven't finished!' shouted Horrid Henry.

'Tough,' said Miss Battle-Axe. 'Now, before we send these autobiographies to the newspaper, I'd like a few of you to read yours aloud to the class. William, let's start with you.'

Weepy William burst into tears. 'I don't want to go first,' he wailed, dabbing his eyes with some loo paper.

'Read,' said Miss Battle-Axe.

WILLIAM'S AUTOBIOGRAPHY

I was born. I cried. A few years later
my brother Neil was born. I cried.
In school Toby broke my pencil.
Margaret picked me last. When we
had to build the Parthenon Henry took
all my paper and then when I got some
more it was dirty. I had to play a blade
of grass in the Nativity play. I cried.
I lost every race on Sports Day.
I cried. Then I got nits. On the school
trip to the Ice Cream Factory I did a
wee in my pants. I cried. Nothing else
has ever happened to me.

'Who's next?' asked Miss Battle-Axe.
Horrid Henry's hand shot up. Miss
Battle-Axe looked as if a zombie had
just walked across her grave. Horrid

Henry never put his hand up.

'Linda,' said Miss Battle-Axe.

Lazy Linda woke up and yawned.

LINDA'S AUTOBIOGRAPHY

I've had many nice beds in my life.
First was my Moses basket. Then
my cot. Then my little bed. Then
my great big sleigh bed. Then my
princess bed with the curtains
and the yellow headboard. I've
also had a lot of duvets. First my

duvet had ducks on it. Then I got a new soft one with big fluffy clouds. Oooh, I am sleepy just thinking about it . . .

'We have time to hear one more,' said Miss Battle-Axe, scanning the class. Horrid Henry thought his arm would detach itself from his shoulder if he shoved it any higher. 'Margaret,' said Miss Battle-Axe.

Henry scowled. It was so unfair. No one wanted to know about that moody old grouch.

Moody Margaret swaggered to the front and noisily cleared her throat.

MARGARET'S AUTOBIOGRAPHY

Greetings, world. I'm very sad when I think that many of you reading this will never get to meet someone as amazing as me. But at least you can read something I've written, and you newspaper people should save this piece of paper, because I, Margaret, have touched it with my very own hands, and it's sure to be valuable in the future when I'm famous.

Let me tell you a few things about marvellous me. First, I am the leader of the Secret Club, which is always victorious against the pathetic and puny Purple Hand Gang next door. One reason we always destroy them, apart from my brilliant plotting, is because the Purple Hand's so-called leader, Henry, is really stupid and useless and pathetic.

Horrid Henry could not believe his ears.

'Liar!' shouted Henry. 'I always win!'

'Shh!' said Miss Battle-Axe.

Naturally, I am the best footballer
the school has ever had or will ever have,
and naturally I'm Captain of the
Football Team. Everyone always
wants to play on my team, but of
course I don't let no-hopers like
Henry on it. I'm also a fantastic
trumpet player, and a top spy.

My best toy is my Dungeon
Drink Kit, which I've used many
times to play great tricks on the
Purple Hand Gang, which they
always fall for.

But I know I'll be very famous
so I'm saving my best stories
for my future best-selling
autobiography. I expect
there will be many statues
built to me all over
town, and that this

school will be renamed the
Margaret School.

I know it's hard realising that you can never
be as great as me, but get used to it!!!

Moody Margaret stopped reading
and swaggered to her seat.

'Yay!' yelled Sour Susan.

'Boo!' yelled Horrid Henry.

'Boo!' yelled Rude Ralph.

'There's no booing in this class,' said
Miss Battle-Axe.

Horrid Henry was outraged.
Margaret's lies about him . . . published?
The Purple Hand Gang always won.
But the whole world would believe
her lies once they read them in a
newspaper. He had to stop that foul
fiend. He had to show everyone what
a pants-face liar Margaret really was.

But how? How? He could just try to
steal her autobiography. But someone
might notice it had gone missing. Or he
could . . . he could . . .

The playtime bell rang. Miss Battle-
Axe starting collecting up all the
autobiographies. Henry watched
helplessly as Margaret's pack of boasting
lies went into the folder.

And then Horrid Henry knew what he had to do. It was dangerous. It was risky. But a pirate gang leader had to take his chances, come what may.

Horrid Henry put up his hand. 'Please, miss, I haven't finished my autobiography yet. Could I stay in at playtime to finish?'

Miss Battle-Axe looked at Henry as if he had just grown an extra head. Henry . . . asking to spend more time on work? Horrid Henry asking to skip playtime?

'You can have five more minutes,' said Miss Battle-Axe, mopping her brow.

Horrid Henry wrote and wrote and wrote. When would Miss Battle-Axe leave him alone for a moment? But there she was, stapling up drawings of light bulbs.

'Put it in the folder with the others,' said Miss Battle-Axe, facing the wall. Horrid Henry didn't wait to be asked twice and grabbed the folder.

There wasn't a moment to lose. Henry rifled through the autobiographies, removed Margaret's, and substituted his new, improved version.

Moody Margaret peered round the door. Tee hee, thought Horrid Henry, pushing past her. Wouldn't she get a

shock when she got her newspaper!
What he'd give to see her face.

THWACK!

The local paper dropped through the
door. Henry snatched it. There was the
headline:

LOCAL CHILDREN SHINE
IN FASCINATING TALES OF
THEIR LIVES

Feverishly, he turned to read the class
autobiographies.

MARGARET'S AUTOBIOGRAPHY

**Oh woe is me, to be such a silly
moody grouchy grump. I've always
looked like a frog, in fact my mum
took one look at me when I was born,
threw me in the bin and ran screaming
from the room. I don't blame her; I
scream too whenever I see my ugly**

warty face in the mirror. Everyone calls me Maggie Moo Moo, or Maggie Poo Poo, because I still wear nappies. I started a Secret Club, which no

one wants to join, because I am so mean and bossy. I can't even have a sleepover without everyone running away. I keep trying to beat Henry's Purple Hand Gang, but he's much too clever for me and always foils my evil plans. I live next door to Henry, but of course I don't deserve such a

great honour. I really should just live in a smelly hole somewhere with all the other frogs. So, just remember, everyone, beware of being a moody, grouchy grump, or you might end up as horrible as me.

Yes! What a triumph! He was brilliant. He was a genius. What an amazing trick to write the truth about Margaret and swap it for her pack of lies.

Horrid Henry beamed. Now to enjoy his own autobiography. It was far too short, but there was always next time.

HENRY'S AUTOBIOGRAPHY

I'm a total copycat. Luckily, I live next door to the amazing Margaret, who I look up to and admire and worship more than anyone in the world. Margaret is my heroine, but I will

never be as clever or as brilliant as she is, because I'm a pathetic, useless toad. I copied her amazing Secret Club, but the Purple Hand always loses. I tried to do Makeovers, but of course I couldn't. Even my own brother wants to work for her as a spy. But then, she is an empress and I'm a worm.

The most exciting thing that ever happened to me was when Margaret moved in next door. I hope that one day she will let me be the guard of the Secret Club, but I will have to work very hard to deserve it. That would be the best thing that has ever happened in my boring life.

Huh? What? That fiend! That foul fiend!

The doorbell rang.

There was Margaret, waving the newspaper. Her face was purple.

'How dare you!' she shrieked.

'How dare you!' Henry shrieked.

'I'll get you for this, Henry,' hissed Margaret.

'Just you wait, Margaret,' hissed Henry.

HORRID HENRY ROCKS

'Boys, I have a very special treat for you,' said Mum, beaming.

Horrid Henry looked up from his *Mutant Max* comic.

Perfect Peter looked up from his spelling homework.

A treat? A special treat? A very special treat? Maybe Mum and Dad were finally appreciating him. Maybe they'd got tickets . . . maybe they'd actually got tickets . . . Horrid Henry's heart leapt. Could it be possible that at last, at long last, he'd get to go to a Killer Boy Rats concert?

'We're going to the Daffy and her Dancing Daisies show!' said Mum. 'I got the last four tickets.'

'OOOOOOHHHH,' said Peter, clapping his hands. 'Yippee! I love Daffy.'

What?? NOOOOOOOOOOOO! That wasn't a treat. That was torture. A treat would be a day at the Frosty Freeze Ice Cream Factory. A treat would be no school. A treat would be all he could eat at Gobble and Go.

'I don't want to see that stupid Daffy,' said Horrid Henry. 'I want to see the Killer Boy Rats.'

'No way,' said Mum.

'I don't like the Killer Boy Rats,' shuddered Peter. 'Too scary.'

'Me neither,' shuddered Mum. 'Too loud.'

'Me neither,' shuddered Dad. 'Too shouty.'

'NOOOOOOOO!' screamed Henry.

'But Henry,' said Peter, 'everyone loves Daffy.'

'Not me,' snarled Henry.

Perfect Peter waved a leaflet. 'Daffy's going to be the greatest show ever. Read this.'

Daffy sings and dances her way across the stage and into your heart. Your chance to sing-along to all your favourite daisy songs! I'm a Lazy Daisy. Whoops-a-Daisy. And of course, Upsy-Daisy, Crazy Daisy, Prance and Dance-a-Daisy.

*

With special guest star Busy Lizzie!!!

AAAAARRRRRGGGGGHHHHHH.

Moody Margaret's parents were taking her to the Killer Boy Rats concert. Rude Ralph was going to the Killer Boy Rats concert. Even Anxious Andrew was going, and he didn't even like them. Stuck-Up Steve had been bragging for months that he was going and would be sitting in a special box. It was so unfair.

No one was a bigger Rats fan than Horrid Henry. Henry had all their albums:
Killer Boy Rats Attack-Tack-Tack,
Killer Boy Rats Splat!
Killer Boy Rats Manic Panic.
'It's not fair!' screamed Horrid Henry. 'I want to see

the Killers!!!!'

'We have to see something that everyone in the family will like,' said Mum. 'Peter's too young for the Killer Boy Rats but we can all enjoy Daffy.'

'Not me!' screamed Henry.

Oh, why did he have such a stupid nappy baby for a brother? Younger brothers should be banned. They just wrecked everything. When he was King Henry the Horrible, all younger brothers would be arrested and dumped in a volcano.

In fact, why wait?

Horrid Henry pounced. He was a fiery god scooping up a human sacrifice and hurling him into the volcano's molten depths.

'AAAIIIIEEEEEEE!' screamed
Perfect Peter. 'Henry attacked me.'

'Stop being horrid, Henry!' shouted
Mum. 'Leave your brother alone.'

'I won't go to Daffy,' yelled Henry.
'And you can't make me.'

'Go to your room,' said Dad.

Horrid Henry paced up and down his
bedroom, singing his favourite Rats
song at the top of his lungs:

I'M dead, you're dead, we're dead.
Get over it.
Dead is great, dead'S where it'S at
'cause . . .

'Henry! Be quiet!' screamed Dad.

'I am being quiet!' bellowed Henry. Honestly. Now, how could he get out of going to that terrible Daffy concert? He'd easily be the oldest one there. Only stupid babies liked Daffy. If the horrible songs didn't kill him then he was sure to die of embarrassment. Then they'd be sorry they'd made him go. But it would be too late. Mum and Dad and Peter could sob and boo hoo all they liked but he'd still be dead. And serve them right for being so mean to him.

Dad said if he was good he could see the Killer Boys next time they were in town. Ha. The Killer Boy Rats

NEVER gave concerts. Next time they did he'd be old and hobbling and whacking Peter with his cane.

He had to get a Killer Boys ticket now. He just had to. But how? They'd been sold out for weeks.

Maybe he could place an ad:

Can you help?
Deserving Boy suffering from rare and terrible illness. His ears are falling off. Doctor has prescribed the Killer Boy Rats cure. Only by hearing the Rats live is there any hope. If you've got a ticket to the concert on Saturday PLEASE send it to Henry NOW.
(If you don't you know you'll be sorry.)

That might work. Or he could tell
people that the concert was cursed and
anyone who went would turn into a
rat. Hmmm. Somehow Henry didn't
see Margaret falling for that. Too bad
Peter didn't have a ticket, thought
Henry sadly, he could tell him he'd turn
into a killer and Peter would hand over
the ticket instantly.

And then suddenly Horrid Henry had a brilliant, spectacular idea. There must be someone out there who was desperate for a Daffy ticket. In fact there must be someone out there who would swap a Killers ticket for a Daffy one. It was certainly worth a try.

'Hey, Brian, I hear you've got a Killer Boy Rats ticket,' said Horrid Henry at school the next day.

'So?' said Brainy Brian.

'I've got a ticket to something much better,' said Henry.

'What?' said Brian. 'The Killers are the best.'

Horrid Henry could barely force the grisly words out of his mouth. He twisted his lips into a smile.

'Daffy and her Dancing Daisies,' said Horrid Henry.

Brainy Brian stared at him.

'Daffy and her Dancing Daisies?' he spluttered.

'Yes,' said Horrid Henry brightly. 'I've heard it's their best show ever. Great new songs. You'd love it. Wanna swap?'

Brainy Brian stared at him as if he had a turnip instead of a head.

'You're trying to swap Daffy and her Dancing Daisies tickets for the Killer Boy Rats?' said Brian slowly.

'I'm doing you a favour, no one likes the Killer Boy Rats any more,' said Henry.

'I do,' said Brian.

Rats.

'How come you have a ticket for Daffy?' said Brian. 'Isn't that a baby show?'

'It's not mine, I found it,' said Horrid Henry quickly. Oops.

'Ha ha Henry, I'm seeing the Killers, and you're not,' Margaret taunted.

'Yeah Henry,' said Sour Susan.

'I heard . . .' Margaret doubled over laughing, 'I heard you were going to the Daffy show!'

'That's a big fat lie,' said Henry hotly. 'I wouldn't be seen dead there.'

Horrid Henry looked around the auditorium at the sea of little baby

nappy faces. There was Needy Neil
clutching his mother's hand. There
was Weepy William, crying because
he'd dropped his ice cream. There was
Toddler Tom, up past his bedtime.
Oh, no! There was Lisping Lily. Henry
ducked.

Phew. She hadn't seen him. Margaret
would never stop teasing him if she ever
found out. When he was king, Daffy
and her Dancing Daisies would live in
a dungeon with only rats for company.
Anyone who so much as mentioned
the name Daffy, or even grew a daisy,
would be flushed down the toilet.

There was a round of polite applause
as Daffy and her Dancing Daisies
pirouetted on stage. Horrid Henry
slumped in his seat as far as he could
slump and pulled his cap over his face.
Thank goodness he'd come disguised

and brought some earplugs. No one would ever know he'd been.

'Tra la la la la la la!' trilled the Daisies. 'Tra la la la la la la!' trilled the audience.

Oh, the torture, groaned Horrid Henry as horrible song followed horrible song. Perfect Peter sang along. So did Mum and Dad.

AAARRRRRGGGHHHHH. And

to think that tomorrow night the Killer
Boy Rats would be performing . . . and
he wouldn't be there! It was so unfair.

Then Daffy cartwheeled to the front
of the stage. One of the daisies stood
beside her holding a giant hat.

'And now the moment all you Daffy
Daisy fans have been waiting for,'
squealed Daffy. 'It's the Lucky Ducky
Daisy Draw, when we call up on stage
an oh-so-lucky audience member to
lead us in the Whoops-a-Daisy sing-along song! Who's it going to be?'

'Me!' squealed Peter. Mum squeezed
his arm.

Daffy fumbled in the hat and pulled
out a ticket.

'And the lucky winner of our ticket
raffle is . . . Henry! Ticket 597! Ticket
597, yes Henry, you in row P, seat 10,
come on up! Daffy needs you on stage!'

Horrid Henry was stuck to his seat in horror. It must be some other Henry. Never in his worst nightmares had he ever imagined—

'Henry, that's you,' said Perfect Peter. 'You're so lucky.'

'Henry! Come on up, Henry!' shrieked Daffy. 'Don't be shy!'

On stage at the Daffy show? No!

No! Wait till Moody Margaret found out. Wait till anyone found out. Henry would never hear the end of it. He wasn't moving. Pigs would fly before he budged.

'Henwy!' squealed Lisping Lily behind him. 'Henwy! I want to give you a big kiss, Henwy . . .'

Horrid Henry leapt out of his seat. Lily! Lisping Lily! That fiend in toddler's clothing would stop at nothing to get hold of him.

Before Henry knew what had happened, ushers dressed as daisies had nabbed him and pushed him on stage.

Horrid Henry blinked in the lights. Was anyone in the world as unlucky as he?

'All together now, everyone get ready to ruffle their petals. Let's sing Tippy-toe daisy do / Let us sing a song for you!' beamed Daffy. 'Henry, you start us off.'

Horrid Henry stared at the vast audience. Everyone was looking at him. Of course he didn't know any stupid Daisy songs. He always blocked his ears or ran from the room whenever Peter sang them. Whatever could the words be . . . 'Watch out, whoop-di-do / Daisy's doing a big poo?'

These poor stupid kids. If only they could hear some decent songs, like . . .

like . . .

**'Granny on her crutches
Push her off her chair
Shove Shove Shove Shove
Shove her down the stairs.'**

shrieked Horrid Henry.

The audience was silent. Daffy looked stunned.

'Uh, Henry . . . that's not Tippy-toe daisy do,' whispered Daffy.

'C'mon everyone, join in with me,' shouted Horrid Henry, spinning round and twirling in his best Killer Boy Rats manner.

'I'm in my coffin
No time for coughin'
When you're squished down dead.
Don't care if you're a boffin
Don't care if you're a loony,
Don't care if you're cartoony
I'll squish you!'

sang Horrid Henry as loud as he could.

'Gonna be a rock star (and you ain't)
Don't even—'

Two security guards ran on stage and grabbed Horrid Henry.

'Killer Boy Rats forever!' shrieked Henry, as he was dragged off.

*

Horrid Henry stared at the special
delivery letter covered in skulls and
crossbones. His hand shook.

Hey Henry,
    We saw a video of you singing our
songs and getting yanked off stage—
way to go, killer boy! Here's a pair of
tickets for our concert tonight, and a
backstage pass—see you there.
            The Killer Boy Rats

Horrid Henry goggled at the tickets and the backstage pass. He couldn't move. He couldn't breathe. He was going to the Killer Boy Rats concert. He was actually going to the Killer Boy Rats concert.

Life, thought Horrid Henry, beaming, was sweet.

ACKNOWLEDGEMENTS

Thanks to Hannah Goodwin, who suggested Horrid Henry's Autobiography would be a good title for a story. And thanks to Michael Rosen for the muddy twig revenge, and to my son Josh, who came up with an extraordinary number of excellent tricks for Henry to play on Peter.

Colour Books

Horrid Henry's Jolly Joke Book
Horrid Henry's Mighty Joke Book
Horrid Henry's Hilariously Horrid Joke Book
Horrid Henry's Purple Hand Gang Joke Book

Early Readers

Don't be Horrid, Henry
Horrid Henry's Birthday Party
Horrid Henry's Holiday
Horrid Henry's Underpants
Horrid Henry Gets Rich Quick
Horrid Henry and the Football Fiend
Horrid Henry's Nits

Horrid Henry is also available on CD and as a digital
download, all read by Miranda Richardson.

'A hoot from beginning to end . . .
As always, Miranda Richardson's delivery is perfection
and the manic music is a delight.'
DAILY EXPRESS

'Long may this dreadful boy continue to terrorise all who
know him. He's a nightmare, but so entertaining . . .
Miranda Richardson's spirited reading is accompanied
by a brilliant music soundtrack – they make a noisy
and fun-filled duo.'
PARENTS' GUIDE

Also by Francesca Simon

HORRiD HENRY

The first book about the adventures of Horrid
Henry, in which Henry tries (unbelievably) to
be good, goes to dance classes, makes 'Glop'
with Moody Margaret and goes on holiday.

'Henry is a truly
great character'
Sunday Times

HORRiD HENRY
Robs the Bank

Horrid Henry helps himself to all the money
he needs to win his favourite board game,
comes up with another spectacular money-
making scheme for launching a newspaper
with all the school gossip, vows vengeance on
Perfect Peter when Peter steals his birthday
party theme and has his own Pirate Party, then
takes over as Head Teacher when Peter plays
school with his goody-goody friends.

HORRiD HENRY
Wakes the Dead

Horrid Henry
finds a sure-fire way of
wielding the remote control
to ensure he always watches his
programme of choice, vies with
Moody Margaret to become the head
of the school, shows off his prowess as
a magician in the school talent show, and
battles it out with Perfect Peter over who
gets the green dinosaur and who gets the
purple one.